The One and Only Me

BY MARILYN SINGER
PICTURES BY NICOLE RUBEL

HarperFestival®
A Division of HarperCollinsPublishers

When Dad and I walk down the street,
Mama says I've got his feet.

When Mom and I choose hats to wear,
Daddy says I've got her hair.

When I read books with Grandma Rose,
Grandpa says I've got her nose.

When Gramps and I pretend we're spies,
Granny says I've got his eyes.

When Peg and I perform headstands,
our brother thinks I've got her hands.

When Ed and I play engineers,
our sister's sure I've got his ears.

When I sing songs with Uncle Keith,
Aunt Lil declares I've got his teeth.

When I dance wild with Aunt Louise,
Uncle Karl points at our knees.

But looking at my family
I know just what I see,

I may have a bit of everyone,
but they all add up to me.

Completely,
uniquely,
definitely,
specially,
the one
and only
ME!